Groundwood Books / House of Anansi Press
110 Spadina Avenue, Suite 801, Toronto, Ontario M5V 2K4
or c/o Publishers Group West
1700 Fourth Street, Berkeley, CA 94710

We acknowledge for their financial support of our publishing program
the Canada Council for the Arts, the Government of Canada through
the Canada Book Fund (CBF) and the Ontario Arts Council.

Canada Council   Conseil des Arts   ONTARIO ARTS COUNCIL
for the Arts   du Canada   CONSEIL DES ARTS DE L'ONTARIO

Library and Archives Canada Cataloguing in Publication
Young, Cybèle
A few blocks / Cybèle Young.
ISBN 978-0-88899-995-5
I. Title.
PS8647.O622F48 2011   jC813'.6   C2011-900508-5

The illustrations were created with ink and watercolor on paper and
cut-out assemblages.
Design by Michael Solomon
Printed and bound in China

For Dave, Calder and Finley

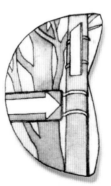

A Few Blocks

Cybèle Young

Groundwood Books   House of Anansi Press   Toronto   Berkeley

It was time for Ferdie and Viola to go to school.
But Ferdie had eleven cars to wash, the highest tower ever to
build and a snake drawing that wasn't done yet.

He didn't want to go to school.
"Not now," he said. "Maybe never. Spike doesn't have to go."

But Viola held out his coat and said, "Ferdie, look! I found your superfast cape! Quick — put on your rocket-blaster boots and we'll take off!"

So up and away they went, speeding faster than the fastest jet,
higher than the highest tower.

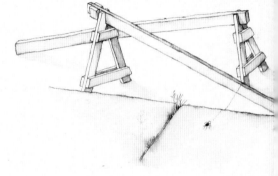

They conquered all evil in their path, until suddenly
Super Ferdinand's rockets ran out of fuel.

Ferdie found a perfect rock and sat down.

"That's it. I'm not going. Not now," he said. "Maybe never."

He watched as some ants on the ground ate a gumdrop.

Viola pointed to a leaf in the gutter and said, "The ship's leaving!
We'd better hop on and go find the buried treasure!"

Captain Ferdinand knew he was an expert navigator, so he
climbed on board.

Bon voyage and out to sea, through fierce thunderstorms.
They swooped over waves higher than mountains,

past speeding dolphins and flying fish, over great blue whales and
giant squid, until…

…they sailed up to an island. On their map X marked the spot.
Sure enough, they dug up treasure.

But just as they were hauling it down to the shore, they saw that
their ship was drifting away.

Ferdie threw himself on the grass, sobbing.

"I won't stop crying! Not now," he said. "Maybe never."

He noticed some clover and began to look for one with four
leaves.

Viola handed him a piece of cardboard and said, "Don't let the
king see you like this. He needs his bravest knight to fight the
fierce fire-breathing dragon who has stolen the princess!"

Sir Ferdinand grabbed his shield and shiny helmet.

Galloping along on his horse, through valleys and past villages, he sped into the kingdom.

He followed the smell of burning wood into the forest, pushed through thickets, crawled through tunnels and stumbled upon some giant twisting trees.

A sooty snort sounded above his head. He saw the princess hanging there, clutched tight in the dragon's claws.

Sir Ferdinand climbed the tree, defeated the dragon and sent him flying.

He had freed the princess, and now he could take her to the palace.

But the princess was tired.

"I'm not going to budge," she said. "Not now. Maybe never."
She thanked the knight for saving her, but she just wanted to be
left alone.

"The king is expecting us!" Sir Ferdinand scolded. But she still wouldn't budge.

He pulled on her hand. That didn't work.

He pushed her. But she just pushed back.

Sir Ferdinand sat down. He sulked. The princess sulked, too.

But then Sir Ferdinand put his hand in his pocket.

He pulled out a magic bean and said, "This will give you superpower strength. You can have half."

So they both got up and walked the last block to school.